We won't
need you
till much,
much later.

Requests for permission to make copies of any part of the work should be mailed to the
following address: Permissions Department, Harcourt, Inc., 6277 Sea Harbor Drive,
Orlando, Florida 32887-6777.

www.harcourt.com

First published in Great Britain in 2000 by Hodder Children's Books
First Red Wagon Books edition 2001

Red Wagon Books is a trademark of Harcourt, Inc., registered
in the United States of America and other jurisdictions.

Library of Congress Cataloging-in-Publication Data
Inkpen, Mick.
Kipper's A to Z: an alphabet adventure/written and illustrated by Mick Inkpen.
p. cm.
Summary: Kipper the dog and his friend Arnold work through the
alphabet by collecting animals and other things for each letter.
[1. Dogs—Fiction. 2. Animals—Fiction. 3. Alphabet.] I. Title.
PZ7.I564Kik 2000
[E]—dc21 00-8853
ISBN 0-15-202594-4

A C E G H F D B

Printed in Mexico

Mick Inkpen

Kipper's

A to Z

Red Wagon Books
Harcourt, Inc.

San Diego   New York   London

This is Kipper's little friend, Arnold. Arnold has found an ant.

A a is for ant.

And Arnold.

Bb is for box

and buzzzzzzzzzzzzzzzzzzzzzzzzzzzzzzzzzzzzzzzzzz

They put the ant
in the box,
and followed
the bumblebee.

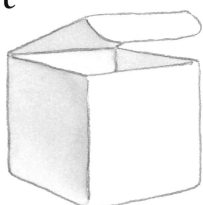

It flew away.

"Let's find something beginning with C," said Kipper.

But the caterpillar had already found them!

Cc is for Crawly caterpillar.

Dd is for duck.

"Duck!" said Arnold.
The duck was too big
to fit into Arnold's box.
And so was the...

enormous

elephant!

Where is the ant?

E e

is for

elephant.

The frog would have
fit in Arnold's box,
but Kipper couldn't
catch it.
It was too fast!

Ff is for frog.

Arnold was still wondering where the ant had gone, when a little green grasshopper jumped straight into his box. "Good!" said Kipper.

G g is for grasshopper.

Hh is for hill and happy.

They skipped all the way to the top

of Big Hill, and down the other side.

Arnold found another
interesting insect.
He opened his box
and put the interesting
insect inside.

I i is for insect.

They went home for
a glass of juice.
Arnold helped himself
to some jam, too.

J j is for juice.

And a bit of jam, too.

Kipper couldn't think of anything beginning with K. Can you think of anything?

Kk is for...

L was easy.
Outside there were
lots of ladybugs.
Lots and lots.
Arnold put one
in his box.

Ll is for

lots of ladybugs.

"Is it my turn now?"
said the zebra.
"No, not now!"
said Kipper.
"You don't
begin with N."

Nn is for
No, not now!

I'm a gnat, and I don't begin with N, either!

Arnold climbed **On** the swing.

O o is for **on**...

And then he fell Off again.

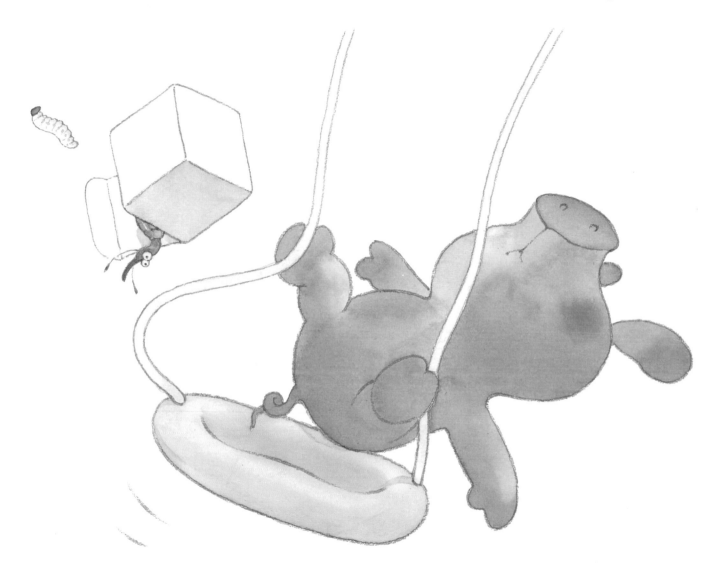

and off.   And oo is for oops!

Arnold was upset.
He sat up puffing and
panting and a little pink.
So Kipper took him to
his favorite place.
The pond.

P p

is for puff, pant, pink,

and pond.

Quack! Quack! Quack!

Quack!

Is that Arnold's ant?

Quack!

Quack!

Quack!

Q q is for quiet!

And quack, of course.

It started to rain.

Rr is for rainbow.

They splashed home
through the puddles.

 S s is for

Splish!

Splosh!

Splash!

And six squishy slugs.

At home Kipper got out his toys.

T t is for toys.

"I know what begins with U!" said Kipper. "Umbrella!"

They played under the umbrella, while the rain poured down outside.

Uu is for

Under the umbrella.

"V is very, very hard," said Kipper. "Do you think we could find a volcano?" Arnold shook his head. So they made a picture of one instead.

V v is for volcano!

The rain stopped.
They looked out the
window to see what
they could see for W.

W w is for

wiggly worm.

But what begins with X?
Kipper thought
and thought
and thought.
He thought of box,
which ends with X, and
he thought of socks,
which doesn't.

"I know!" he said
suddenly. Kipper picked
up the interesting insect.

Xx is for

Xugglybug!

"It must be my turn
by now!" said the zebra.
"Is it my turn?
Is it?
Is it?"

Yy is for

Yes!

So the zebra stood
in the middle of the page,
and we all said,

Z z is for Zebra!

ZZZZZZZZZZZZZZZZZZZZZZZZ
ZZZZ
ZZZ
ZZ
ZZ
ZZZ
ZZZZ
ZZZZZZZZZZZZZZZZZZZZ
ZZZZ
ZZ
Z

zzzzzzzz

And for Arnold's little Zoo, too.